"I could almost smell the blood in the air. Its coppery scent almost palpable on my tongue."

"It was still warm, having just gushed forth from the animal's ruptured heart. It was beautiful."

EXACTLY. BUT EVEN *WITH* A BULLET IN HIM, HE GAVE US A *DEVIL* OF A RUN FOR IT.

WELL, IT WAS *MANNY* HERE, WHO FINALLY PUT IT *DOWN.* EVEN AS THE THING WAS *ATTACKING.* WHAT A *SHOT.*

MAGNIFICENT.

MY BROTHER *EXAGGERATES.* IT WAS A *LUCKY* SHOT. THE VERY ONE THAT SPOOKED YOUR *HORSE,* I'M AFRAID.

THE *HEAD* WILL MAKE A FINE *TROPHY,* HERR *RICHTHOFEN.*

BUT THE *KILL* IS RIGHTFULLY *YOURS* COUNTESS. THIS IS *YOUR* LAND.

I *INSIST* YOU HAVE IT. LET IT BE A *REMINDER* OF YOUR FIRST VISIT TO OUR COUNTRY.

THANK YOU, MADAM. I AM *HONORED.*

WHEREAS, IF YOUR GUIDES WILL DELIVER THE CARCASS TO MY *CASTLE,* I WOULD INVITE YOU ALL TO *DINNER* TOMORROW NIGHT TO FEAST ON YOUR *SPOILS.*

ALAS, MADAM, I AM AFRAID WE MUST *REGRETFULLY* DECLINE YOUR *GENEROUS* INVITATION. WE MUST CATCH THE MIDNIGHT TRAIN TO *PRAGUE* THIS VERY NIGHT.

IS THERE *NOTHING* I CAN DO TO ALTER YOUR PLANS? *SURELY* ANOTHER DAY WILL NOT MATTER SO *CRUCIALLY?*

UNFORTUNATELY IT DOES. I HAVE RECENTLY BEEN *PROMOTED* AND MUST REPORT TO MY NEW COMMAND AT FIRST LIGHT.

AH, YOU ARE A *SOLDIER.* I SHOULD HAVE GUESSED. IN WHAT *BRANCH* DO YOU SERVE, HERR RICHTHOFEN,... THE *CAVALRY,* PERHAPS?

"His smile and laughter were infections. It had been a long time since anyone had made me laugh."

HA, HA, HA.

WHY, *YES,* I AM... *OH!* OF *COURSE.* HA, HA.

GOOD *NIGHT,* COUNTESS.

AND TO *YOU* AS WELL, *SIR.* A SAFE JOURNEY TO YOU *ALL.*

AU REVOIR, DEAR LADY. DUTY CALLS.

"He was so brutally handsome. Even in his innocence, I wanted him. It was a longing both strange and intoxicating."

PERHAPS WE SHALL MEET *AGAIN* SOME DAY

I WOULD LIKE THAT VERY *MUCH,* HERR RICHTHOFEN. VERY MUCH *INDEED.*

"Watching him ride off, I vowed to one day find him again; no matter what the cost or how long it would take."

DAMN IT, MANNY, BUT YOU HAVE *ALL* THE LUCK. WE GO HUNTING FOR *PIGS* AND YOU END UP RESCUING A BEAUTIFUL *COUNTESS.*

WHY LITTLE *BROTHER,* I THOUGHT YOU *KNEW,* SOME MEN ARE SIMPLY *BORN* TO DO GREAT DEEDS. ISN'T THAT *RIGHT,* FATHER?

IN *YOUR* CASE I BELIEVE IT *IS.* OR SO YOUR *MOTHER* KEEPS TELLING ME. HA!

"For what is time to one who is immortal?"

"Feverish with thoughts of him, I hurried back to the castle just as a northern gust heralded a change in the weather."

"My major domo, Jorgen, greeted me with his usual stoic charm."

YOU ARE *LATE.* WAS THERE ANY *TROUBLE?*

JUST UNEXPECTED *COMPANY* ALONG THE TRAIL. IS EVERY-THING READY IN MY *ROOM?*

GOOD. MY HUNGER IS *STRONG* TONIGHT.

IRENA HAS IT *PREPARED.*

I HAVE A *MISSION* FOR YOU.

YES, MISTRESS.

AT FIRST LIGHT, YOU ARE TO CALL MY *LAWYER* IN *ZURICH* AND TELL HIM I WISH A *DETAILED* REPORT ON A GERMAN FAMILY NAMED *RICHTHOFEN.*

IN PARTICULAR THE *SON, MANFRED.*

TELL HIM THERE WILL BE A *GENEROUS* BONUS FOR HIM IF I HAVE IT WITHIN THE *WEEK.*

AS YOU *WISH.*

"The evening's events had heightened my needs to a fever pitch and seeing Drena only inflamed them."

IT'S ABOUT *TIME.*

WATCH YOUR *TONGUE,* I AM IN *NO MOOD* FOR IT. TELL ME ABOUT WHAT YOU'VE *BROUGHT* ME, AND BE *QUICK* ABOUT IT*!*

"I could sense the fear coming from beyond the door and it aroused me."

HE'S SOME KIND OF *BOTANIST.* THE MEN FOUND HIM CHASING *BUTTERFLIES* OUT BY THE RIVER. HE HAD THESE BIG *NETS...*

ENOUGH! LEAVE ME!

"The man on my bed looked strong and virile, much to my relief. On this night I craved blood filled with energy and life."

"All that was left was to play out the ritual as I had done countless times before."

⑩

There is a connection between love and death stronger than all the powers of the universe."

"It lies just under the skin like a network of lust and fire..."

"...and even the fear of death cannot dim its wanting."

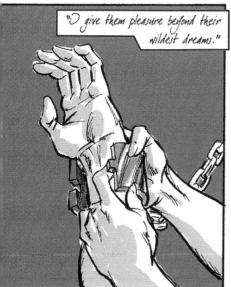

"I give them pleasure beyond their wildest dreams."

MAKE LOVE TO ME.

"Long ago I stopped tormenting myself with the right or wrong of it."

"I give, I take and I go on. There was never anything more... until that night."

"That night I was unsettled and confused. All Because of my encounter with young Manfred Von Richthofen."

"He would fill my dreams from that moment on."

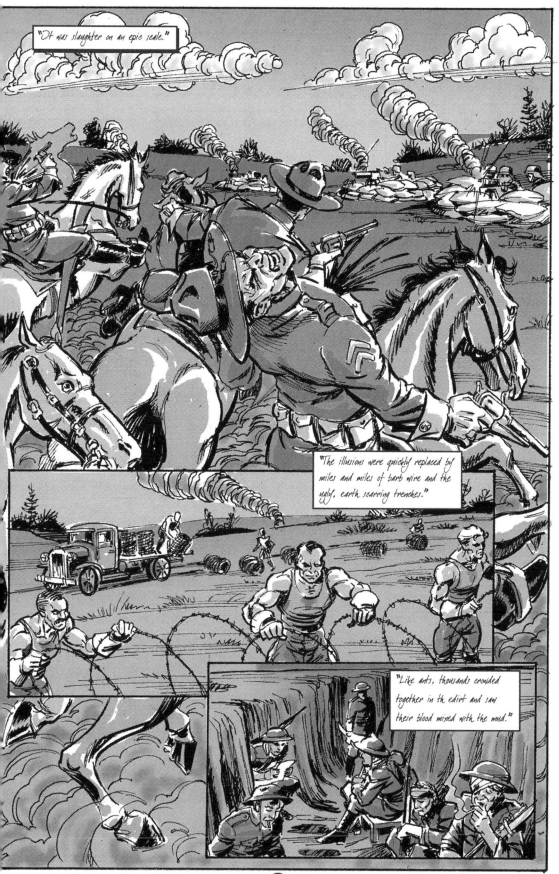

"It was slaughter on an epic scale."

"The illusions were quickly replaced by miles and miles of barb wire and the ugly, earth scarring trenches."

"Like ants, thousands crowded together in th edirt and saw their blood mixed with the mud."

"With the world a living Hell, a few daring warriors turned their gaze skyward to the heavens."

"One of these was my Lt. Von Riethofen, who, according to my sources, met the famous pilot, Oswald Boelcke in early 1915."

"From that point on, he was committed to becoming a flier."

"He made his first solo flight on October 15th of that same year and capped the occasion..."

"...by crashing during his landing."

"This near brush with death would have paralyzed most men, but not this brash daredevil. Instead it only whetted his appetite for more."

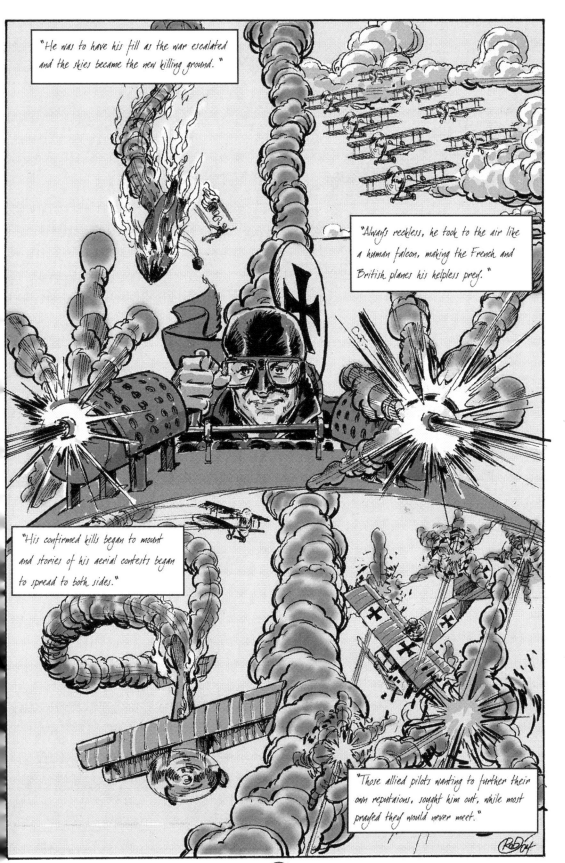

"He was to have his fill as the war escalated and the skies became the new killing ground."

"Always reckless, he took to the air like a human falcon, making the French and British planes his helpless prey."

"His confirmed kills began to mount and stories of his aerial contests began to spread to both sides."

"Those allied pilots wanting to further their own reputaisons, sought him out, while most prayed they would never meet."

It was all a big game for Manfred and he seemed invincible in his sky chariot.

For the first time in his life, Manfred experienced pain & loss...

Then in October of 1916, after 40 victories, Boelcke was killed in a mid-air collision with one of his own wing mates.

...and from that moment on, everything changed.

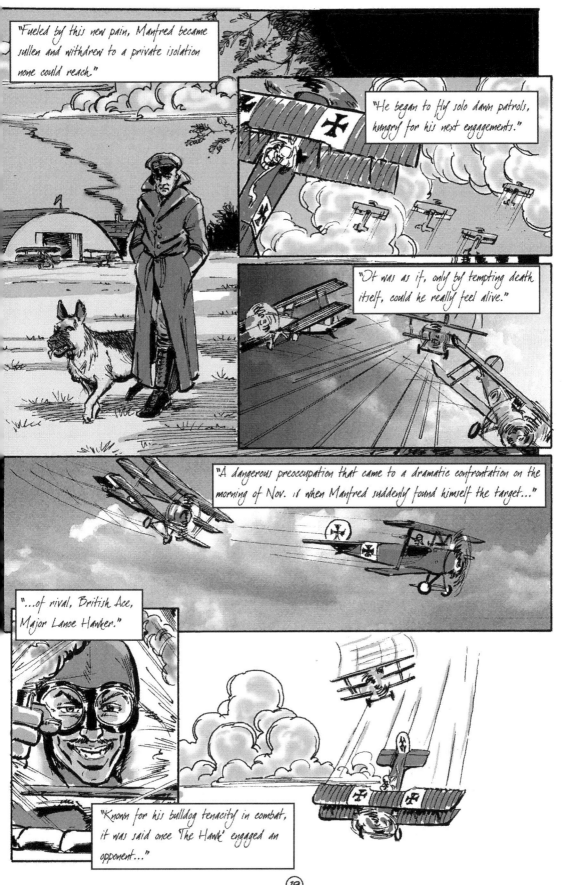

"Fueled by this new pain, Manfred became sullen and withdrew to a private isolation none could reach."

"He began to fly solo dawn patrols, hungry for his next engagements."

"It was as if, only by tempting death itself, could he really feel alive."

"A dangerous preoccupation that came to a dramatic confrontation on the morning of Nov. 11 when Manfred suddenly found himself the target..."

"...of rival, British Ace, Major Lanoe Hawker."

"Known for his bulldog tenacity in combat, it was said once 'The Hawk' engaged an opponent..."

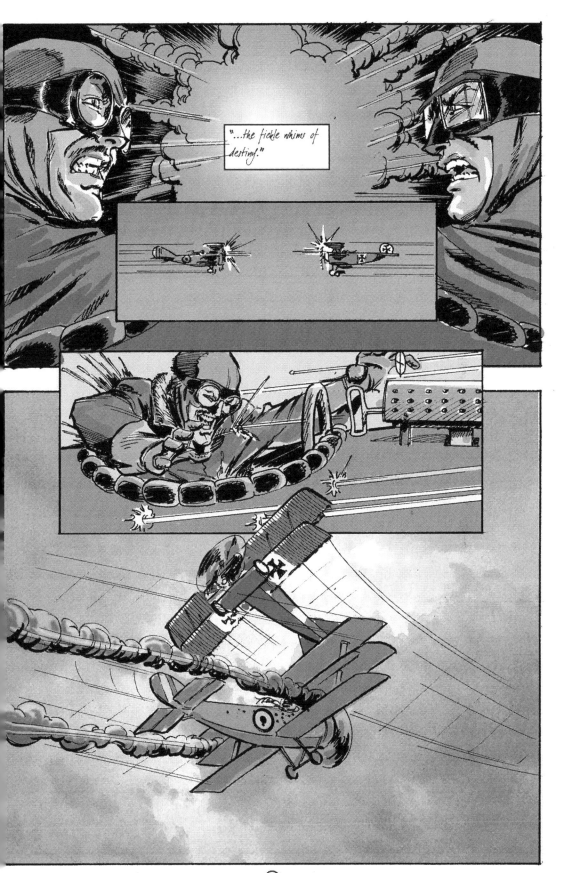

"...the fickle whims of destiny."

"Thus did his reputation continue to swell like an oncoming tide from which there was no escape."

"January 1917. My years of waiting & watching from afar are over."

Kreuzzeitung

12 January 1917

FLYING ACE AWARDED BLUE MAX

EXCELLENT. HE HAS BECOME ALL I ENVISIONED, MY YOUNG *HERO.*

JORGEN, WE WILL BE GOING TO *BERLIN.* SEE TO IT THAT ALL IS MADE READY. I WISH TO DEPART AS *SOON* AS *POSSIBLE.*

YES, MISTRESS. I WILL SEE TO IT.

IT IS *TOO FAR.*

IT IS TOO *DANGEROUS* FOR YOU.

I WILL BE THE JUDGE OF THAT, IRENA.

WHAT IS SO *IMPORTANT* ABOUT THIS ONE? HE'S JUST A *MAN.*

NO, HE IS *NOT.* HE IS *DIFFERENT.* I SENSED IT IN HIM THE NIGHT WE *MET* AND HE HAS PROVEN ME *CORRECT.*

BAH! YOU SOUND LIKE SOME LOVE SICK *SCHOOL GIRL.* IT IS A *FOOLISH* OBSESSION AND IT HAS *BLINDED* YOU.

REALLY? HOW SO?

YOUR KIND IS *INCAPABLE* OF LOVE. IT IS SOMETHING FOR THE *LIVING.*

"She was once called the Athens on the Spree, this city torn between two worlds..."

"...that of war and peace, old and new. This Berlin."

"But there was no doubts as to her new conqueror."

LOOK, EVERYONE! HE'S HERE!

IT'S VON RICHTHOFEN AND HIS BROTHER.

OH, LOOK, HE'S WEARING IT, THE BLUE MAX.

HE'S SO HANDSOME. I MUST MEET HIM.

CLAP!

CLAP!

CLAP!

Hoorah!

Bravo!

WELCOME, HERR VON RICHTHOFEN. IT IS AN HONOR TO HAVE YOU JOIN US!

BULL. YOU LOVE EVERY MINUTE OF IT.

HERE WE GO AGAIN.

EVERYONE IS SIMPLY DYING TO MEET YOU.

THANK YOU, HERR KOHLER. I HOPE I DON'T DISAPPOINT THEM TOO GREATLY.

"Then for the very first time, he took me in his arms and whirled me across the floor."

"The band was playing a Strauss melody and my heart soared with each lovely strain."

"It was as close to Heaven as I will be allowed."

IT'S *INCREDIBLE.* YOU ARE AS *YOUNG* AND *BEAUTIFUL* AS THAT DAY IN THE *WOODS.* WHAT WITCHCRAFT *IS* THIS?

HA. DO YOU *REALLY* WANT AN *ANSWER* OR WOULD YOU RATHER NOT ENJOY THE *MYSTERY* THAT I AM?

THERE IS NOTHING *ABOUT* YOU WHICH IS *NOT* A MYSTERY. YOU'RE LIKE A *SHADOW* ON THE *MOON.*

AND *YOU,* SIR ARE AS SKILLED WITH *WORDS* AS YOU ARE WITH *AIRPLANES.*

ONLY WHEN THEY WILL WIN ME THAT WHICH I *DESIRE.*

AND WHAT *IS* IT YOU... *DESIRE?*

CLAP! CLAP! CLAP!

I BELIEVE THE MUSIC HAS *STOPPED.*

WHAT...? OH... OF COURSE.

IT IS SO *STIFLING.*

PERHAPS SOME *FRESH AIR* IS IN ORDER.

MY THOUGHTS *EXACTLY.* LEAD ON, SIR.

LOTHAR, OFFER MY *APOLOGIES* TO OUR HOST, *WILL YOU?*

YOU'RE *LEAVING?* WHAT SHALL I *SAY?*

TELL THEM I WAS CALLED *AWAY* ON A TOP SECRET MISSION. *ANY-THING.* I DON'T *CARE.* I'LL SEE YOU BACK AT THE BARRACKS.

YOUR BROTHER IS ONE *LUCKY DEVIL.*

HMM, I WONDER.

CABBIE! ARE YOU *FREE?*

"The night air on my skin was intoxicating. I was alive with sensations."

AT YOUR *SERVICE,* SIR?

29

Then we would return to my apartments on Zirkus Strabe and I would become the teacher.

Together we explored our bodies like erotic voyagers...

... each trying to outdo the other with these...

...delicious thrills of the flesh.

And when we were done, there was always the sweet surrender into a dreamless sleep.

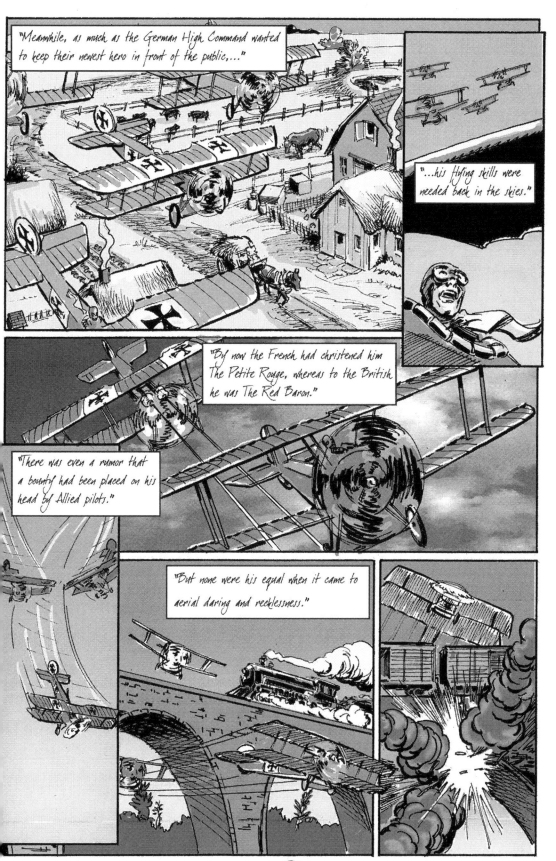

"Meanwhile, as much as the German High Command wanted to keep their newest hero in front of the public,..."

"...his flying skills were needed back in the skies."

"By now the French had christened him The Petite Rouge, whereas to the British he was The Red Baron."

"There was even a rumor that a bounty had been placed on his head by Allied pilots."

"But none were his equal when it came to aerial daring and recklessness."

LOTHAR, *THERE* YOU ARE! HOW WAS *THAT* FOR A CLOSE CALL, *HEH*?

YOU THINK NEARLY *DYING* WAS SOME KIND OF *LAUGHING MATTER*?

COME *ON*, LITTLE BROTHER, WHAT'S THE...

STOP IT! STOP ACTING LIKE IT'S ALL A BIG *GAME*!

EVER SINCE YOU TOOK UP WITH *THAT WOMAN*, YOU'VE BEEN A *WRECK*!

YOU COME IN EVERY MORNING LOOKING LIKE SOMETHING THE *DAMN CAT* DRAGGED IN. *THEN* YOU GO *UP THERE* AND MAKE MISTAKES!

FOOLISH, IDIOTIC MISTAKES THAT ARE GOING TO GET YOU *KILLED*!

I *SEE. THAT'S* HOW IT IS. YOU THINK MY RELATIONSHIP WITH *MARYA* IS WRONG.

THERE IS SOMETHING *STRANGE* ABOUT HER. SHE'S *BEWITCHING* YOU SOMEHOW.

WHY, BECAUSE SHE IS *BEAUTIFUL* AND I AM FALLING IN *LOVE* WITH HER? IS THAT SO *UNNATURAL*?

OR THE FACT THAT SHE CAN ONLY SEE YOU AT *NIGHT*. WHAT DOES SHE DO WITH HER *DAYS*?

NO, THERE'S MORE TO IT. HOW DO YOU EXPLAIN THE FACT SHE DOESN'T APPEAR TO HAVE *AGED* SINCE WE FIRST MET HER FIVE YEARS AGO?

FOR *HEAVEN'S SAKE*, *LISTEN* TO YOURSELF.

WE MET *MARYA* ON AN *UNLIT* COUNTRY ROAD IN THE MIDDLE OF THE *NIGHT*. HOW CAN YOU REMEMBER SO WELL HER *LOOK* OR EVEN GUESS HER *AGE* FROM THAT *ONE* ENCOUNTER?

I DON'T

ALL *I* RECALL WAS A *VERY* BEAUTIFUL WOMAN WHO SEEMS TO HAVE GOTTEN EVEN *LOVELIER*.

"Four of these on the same day, April 29th, a personal best."

"After his 41st victory, he was ordered to leave and turn over command to Lothar."

"He spent his vacation hunting in his home town..."

"...and travelling on propaganda tours with Kaiser Wilhelm. The people adored him."

VICTORY

"Unable to remain completely idle, Manfred sought out aircraft designer, Anthony Fokker, and together they plan the development of a new and faster warbird, the DR.1 Triplane."

"On June 24th he returned to war and was given command of the newly formed Fighter Wing 1."

"But his joy was to be short lived, for two weeks later, he was nearly killed..."

"...when hit by a bullet to the head."

"Only through his indomitable strength of will did he manage to land in one piece."

"He was rushed to a nearby field hospital and miraculously recovered."

"Terrified that they might actually lose their number one propaganda hero, the High Command once again placed him on inactive duty."

"He was sent to a Military Hospital in Hamburg, there to remain until he was fully fit for duty."

"Realizing his arguments would be futile, he reluctantly agreed."

COME *ALONG,* GIRL. THE SUN IS ALMOST *GONE* AND WE DON'T WANT TO BE OUT HERE WHEN IT GETS *DARK.*

WOF! WOF!

WHAT *IS* IT, GIRL? IS THERE SOMETHING *OUT THERE?*

GRRRRRR!

ONLY A *FRIEND,* IF YOU *NEED* ONE.

"The following night it was as if we had never been apart. So easily did we fall back into the intimacy of being together."

THANK YOU, IRENA. DINNER WAS DELICIOUS. AFTER THAT *HORRIBLE MESS* THEY DISH OUT AT THE *HOSPITAL*, IT IS A *WONDER* ANYONE CAN EVER GET BETTER.

YOU ARE *MOST* KIND, *HERR RICHTHOFEN.* I AM *HAPPY* THE MEAL WAS TO YOUR *SATISFACTION.*

IRENA IS A *TREASURE.* I WOULD BE *LOST* WITHOUT HER.

"My heart was bursting with happiness again. Perhaps too much happiness for such as I."

MY, BUT YOU PLAY *BEAUTIFULLY.* WHAT *OTHER* SECRETS ARE YOU KEEPING FROM ME, *MY DEAR?*

PLEASE DON'T LEAVE ME AGAIN. *PROMISE* ME. I COULDN'T *BEAR* TO BE WITHOUT YOU AGAIN. *EVER!*

MARYA, WHAT'S THE *MATTER?* YOU'RE *SHAKING.*

"The words bubbled from my lips, free and unchained."

OH, *MANNY,* I LOVE YOU *SO* MUCH. SOMETIMES IT *HURTS.*

AND I, *YOU,* MY *BEAUTIFUL* ONE. FROM THE FIRST MOMENT I *SAW* YOU. DO NOT BE AFRAID, I WILL *NEVER* LEAVE YOU.

"Before I realized what I was doing, I plunged further into my madness of love."

WHY NOT **LEAVE** THE HOSPITAL AND COME STAY HERE WITH ME? I'M **SURE** BETWEEN IRENA AND MYSELF, WE COULD SEE TO YOUR CARE.

WHAT A **SPLENDID** IDEA. I'LL TELL THE AD-MINISTRATOR **FIRST THING** TOMORROW MORNING. BUT ARE YOU **SURE**? THIS IS WHAT YOU **REALLY** WANT?

MORE THAN **ANYTHING.**

THEN CONSIDER IT **DONE.**

HAVE YOU LOST YOUR **SENSES.** COUNTESS?

PERHAPS I **HAVE,** IRENA. WHEN I'M WITH HIM, I JUST CAN'T THINK OF **ANYTHING ELSE.** IS THAT SO **WRONG**?

AND WHAT WILL WE **TELL** HIM WHEN HE WAKES UP IN THE **MORNING** AND YOU ARE NOT BY HIS SIDE?

HOW WILL WE EXPLAIN YOUR **ABSENSE** EVERY DAY?

I DON'T **KNOW.** AND I DON'T **CARE.** YOU AND JORGEN WILL DO **WHATEVER** IT TAKES TO MAKE THIS **WORK.** IS THAT **PERFECTLY** CLEAR?

PERFECTLY.

GOOD. I WILL **RETIRE** NOW, **JORGEN,** I WILL LEAVE IT TO **YOU** TO ASSIST THE CAPTAIN WHEN HE ARRIVES TOMORROW.

YES, **COUNTESS.** I WILL SEE HE IS MADE COM-FORTABLE.

THANK YOU, **BOTH** OF YOU.

"It was insanity to think I could deceive Manfred forever. Of course, poor Irena and Jorgen did their best under the circumstances."

WILL SHE BE GONE *LONG?*

THE COUNTESS HAD SOME URGENT *BUSINESS* IN TOWN. SHE *APOLOGIZES* FOR NOT BEING HERE TO *WELCOME* YOU *PROPERLY.*

MOST OF THE *DAY,* I'M AFRAID. *COME,* CAPTAIN, LET ME SHOW YOU TO YOUR ROOMS

"Thus began our daily charade built on a frame of flimsy and ridiculous lies."

MARYA! AT LAST!

"I wonder at times if he ever believed any of them."

MYSTERIOUS AS EVER, AREN'T YOU? BUT WHAT AM I TO *DO* ALL DAY *WITHOUT* YOU?

USE YOUR *IMAGINATION,* DARLING. THINK OF OUR *NIGHTS* TOGETHER.

FORGIVE ME, *DEAREST.* I HOPE YOU WEREN'T *TOTALLY* BORED. I'M AFRAID THESE TRIPS ARE *VITAL.*

AND *WHAT,* PRAY TELL, WILL *THOSE* ENTAIL?

EVERY *NASTY LITTLE THING* YOUR *DIRTY LITTLE MIND* CAN *DREAM* OF... *DEAR.*

SUDDENLY, I'M VERY *HUNGRY...*

... AND *NOT...* FOR *DINNER.*

"At first it was like Berlin. Our mutual need for each other. Each night making us slaves to our all consuming desires."

"Still, Manfred's condition gave me pause and lent restraint to my demands."

"Gradually, his strength returned as did his ardor and once more we were engaged in a brutal, carnal journey of discovery."

"I knew it would never last and I was right."

"It was early Autumn and the leaves had started to change their colors. The night air was crisp and clear."

"It amplified even the faintest sounds..."

SNAP

"...like the blast of a cannon."

"I could sense them even as they came over the courtyard wall. Their hearts pounding away like drums in their heaving breasts."

"There were four of them. Allied assassins sent to murder the man their pilots could not defeat."

"It was child's play."

BRANDY, SIR?

YES, JORGEN. THANK YOU.

AS YOU *WISH*, MISTRESS. WILL THERE BE ANY-THING *ELSE*?

NO, JORGEN. THAT WILL BE *ALL* FOR NOW, THANK YOU.

TELL IRENA WE WILL BE READY *SHORTLY*.

HE AND IRENA ARE *DEVOTED* TO YOU, AREN'T THEY?

YES, THEIR *LOYALTY* IS UNQUESTIONED.

BOTH OF THEM ARE FROM THE VILLAGE NEAR *CASTLE DRACULA* BACK HOME.

IT IS PART OF THE *ARRANGEMENT* MY FATHER HAD WITH THEM. ABOUT OUR... BEING *VAMPIRES*.

MARYA, YOU DON'T *HAVE* TO SAY ANY *MORE*. IRENA TOLD ME ABOUT YOUR... *HUNGER*.

NO, DARLING. THAT IS NOT *ENOUGH*. I HAVE TO TELL YOU... *EVERY-THING*. FROM THE BEGINNING.

66

"He was an attentive audience, as I related the singular history of House Dracula."

"How in 1462 the Mongol Turks swept across the mid-eastern Rumanias bent on the total conquest of the Christian empire."

"My father, a knight in the order of St. George, watched his armies slaughtered in battle after battle."

"Thinking that God had betrayed him, he lashed out at the church itself, cursing the very crucifix he had once defended."

"He offered his allegiance to Satan and all the dark principalities if it would bring him victory and save his country."

"Before fleeing, a company of Mongols attacked the castle and butchered all within."

"My mother and brothers all dead before him."

"Even I had not been spared their animal lust for vengeance and lay twisted and broken at the age of twelve before my father's tortured eyes."

"Then he did the only thing he could to save me."

"He gave me the kiss of the vampire."

"Thus began our journey through time together as the last of the Draculas."

"After the war, the people of the village pledged themselves to us in gratitude for what my father had done."

THEY VOWED TO SERVE US *LOYALLY* AS LONG AS WE WALKED THE EARTH AND TO THIS DAY THEY, AND THEIR *DESCENDANTS*, SUCH AS *IRENA* AND *JORGEN*, HAVE KEPT THAT PROMISE FAITHFULLY.

WHAT AN *INCREDIBLE* TALE BUT *1462...?* THAT MAKES YOU WELL... OVER...

FOUR HUNDRED AND FIFTY FIVE TO BE *EXACT.* I HOPE YOU HAVE A TASTE FOR *OLDER WOMEN* MY DEAR. *HA.*

ONLY *ONE* IN PARTICULAR. BUT MARYA, WHAT HAPPENED TO YOUR *FATHER,* THE *COUNT?*

HE'S *DEAD.*

BUT *HOW?* I THOUGHT YOU SAID YOU COULD NOT DIE?

OH, THERE *ARE* WAYS TO KILL US. A *STAKE* TO THE *HEART, HOLY WATER* OR THE *RAYS* OF THE *SUN.*

BUT THE *WORST* IS THE ONE WE INFLICT UPON OURSELVES.

I'M AFRAID I DON'T UNDERSTAND

IT'S THE *LONELINESS.* THE *AGONY* OF SEEING ALL THE PEOPLE YOU *EVER* LOVED AND *CARED* FOR GROW *OLD* AND *DIE* WHILE YOU SIMPLY CONTINUE.

ALWAYS *ALONE.*

MY FATHER *TRIED* TO RELIEVE HIS LONELINESS WITH *TRAVEL.* .

WHILE IN ENGLAND, MANY YEARS AGO, HE MET A WOMAN THERE WHO REMINDED HIM OF MY MOTHER

HIS LOVE FOR HER *BLINDED* HIM TO THE DANGERS OF SUCH A DECLARATION.

WHEN HER FAMILY DISCOVERED HIS *TRUE* IDENTITY, THEY SOUGHT OUT HIS COFFIN AND ... THEY DROVE A *STAKE* THROUGH HIS *HEART.*

MARYA, I'M *SO SORRY.* IT MUST HAVE BEEN SO *HARD* FOR YOU AFTER THAT.

I *CONSOLED* MYSELF WITH THE THOUGHT THAT HE WAS AT *LONG LAST* AT *PEACE.* I EVEN *ENVIED* HIM.

"He took me in his arms and I knew my life would never be the same. For the first time I began to see the power of his love."

NOR *I*, MY DARLING

"Once committed, Manfred demanded that we begin his transformation immediately. That night I explained the ritual to him, nervous that his determination might waver at the last moment."

FOR THE PROCESS TO *WORK*, I MUST DRAIN YOUR BLOOD THREE TIMES IN THE NEXT NINE MONTHS.

BUT WON'T THAT *KILL* ME?

NOT *IMMEDIATELY*. DURING THE FIRST AND SECOND KISSES, I WILL *CEASE* IN TIME FOR YOU TO RECOVER FROM THE LOSS.

I *SEE*. AND THE *THIRD*?

"When it was over, he lay perilously close to death. His brave heart barely beating, as his body fought off the shock of my attack."

"Prayers, alien to my tongue, leapt forth in the stillness around us as if uttered by a stranger."

PLEASE GOD, DO NOT TAKE THIS FROM ME.

COME, MISTRESS. DAWN IS ONLY HOURS AWAY. YOU MUST REST NOW.

YOU WILL LOOK AFTER HIM, WON'T YOU?

I SWEAR I WILL NOT LEAVE HIS SIDE. WHEN HE IS ABLE, THERE IS SOUP IN THE KITCHEN TO HELP REBUILD HIS STRENGTH.

NOW GO, OR YOU WILL BE OF NO USE TO HIM EITHER.

THANK YOU, IRENA.

GO ON NOW! SHOO! GET YOUR SLEEP. YOU WILL NEED ALL YOUR WITS ABOUT YOU IN THE NEXT FEW DAYS.

"Of all the times I had left him, this was the most wrenching. But Irena was right, as always."

"To my utter relief, Manfred recovered speedily. Within days he was sitting up and joking again."

"We returned to a relaxed, intimate routine, simply content to be in each other's presence."

"For a while we almost forgot the outside world and its madness. But only for a while."

I'LL BE BACK IN THREE WEEKS. *TRUST ME*, MY DEAR. YOU'LL SEE. IT *WILL* HAPPEN.

YES, I KNOW, MY LOVE. BUT ALLOW A WOMAN'S RIGHT TO WORRY EVEN A *LITTLE*.

"And once more he was gone. Back to his endless blue sky and his destiny."

"By the time Manfred rejoined his command, it was late August and the new Fokker DR.1 triplanes had arrived."

"He ordered his painted cherry red from cowl to tail."

"On the first of September, he scored his sixtieth victory: his first in the DR.1."

"Though he actually flew biplanes most of his career, it was with the red triplane that he forever became associated as the Red Baron."

"Whereas I closed up the house in Germany and returned to Castle Dracula to await his next leave."

"The following few nights we spent enjoying the Winter countryside draped in its mantle of pure white snow."

"Once again Chateau Dracula came alive with the music of human laughter and gaiety."

"It was the happiest time of my life."

"As the hours of his leave ticked by, each moment together became a fragile treasure."

I NEVER WANT YOU TO LEAVE ME AGAIN. *EVER*.

OH, *MARYA*. SOON IT WILL BE FINISHED. BOTH THIS RIDICULOUS *WAR* AND OUR TIME APART.

I *PROMISE* YOU.

"There was nothing I would not have done for him."

IRENA WILL NOT LET HIM SLIP AWAY. BESIDES, HIS LOVE FOR YOU IS MUCH STRONGER THAN DEATH.

YOU ARE AN INCURABLE ROMANTIC, OLD WOMAN.

NO, I AM A *REALIST.* THERE IS NO FORCE IN THIS WORLD STRONGER THAN LOVE. EVEN THE CURSE ON THIS HOUSE CANNOT COMPLETELY SUBDUE IT.

AS *YOU* WELL KNOW.

TOUCHÈ.

I MUST RETIRE NOW. *THANK YOU,* IRENA.

GO, MISTRESS. WHEN YOU AWAKEN, HE WILL BE BETTER.

"As I left them, I felt a weariness that was alien to me."

"For the first time in my unholy existence, I came to my coffin tired and needing its promise of rest."

"As I closed my eyes, the cares of my lovesick heart seemed to evaporate as I slept."

84

"My brave Manfred did recover, but it was a slow, delicate process."

WHAT WOULD YOU LIKE ME TO PLAY NEXT, DEAREST?

PLAY THAT STRAUSS WALTZ WE DANCED TO IN BERLIN.

YOUR *COFFEE*, CAPTAIN. I TOOK THE LIBERTY OF ADDING A LITTLE BIT OF *BRANDY*.

YOU ARE A *TREASURE* AS WELL AS A *BEAUTY*, MADAM. I DRINK TO YOUR GOOD HEALTH AND FORTUNE.

AND *YOU* ARE A *SILVER* TONGUED *DEVIL*, YOU ARE. *HEE HEE*.

MANNY, I AM GETTING *JEALOUS* OF ALL THIS ATTENTION TO MY *MAID*.

AS WELL YOU *SHOULD*, MY DEAR. THE WOMAN IS A *NYMPH* WITH THE MOST *MARVELOUS* MASSAGING HANDS.

BAH! YOU ARE *DEPRAVED!* *BOTH* OF YOU!

IRENA! COME BACK, PLEASE!

NOW SEE WHAT YOU'VE *DONE*.

SHE JUST MIGHT LEAVE FOR *GOOD* IF YOU KEEP *TEASING* HER LIKE THAT.

HA, HA, HA, HA.

OH, *COME* MY DEAR. SHE LOVES EVERY BIT OF IT.

BESIDES, YOU *KNOW* SHE IS TOTALLY DEVOTED TO YOU.

REALLY? AND IS THERE ANYONE *ELSE* IN THIS CASTLE SO INCLINED IN MY FAVOR?

GUESS.

"The details are recorded in the history texts. Cold, un-feeling facts about his final days."

"It was as if the fates conspired against us."

"Still weak from the draining, he began to suffer recurring headaches and bouts of dizziness."

"Then Lothar was severely wounded in mid-April, thus robbing Manfred of his most experienced and valuable wingman."

"Thus, on April 21st, while in the course of a normal sortie, Manfred engaged a British Sopwith Camel flown by Wilfred May."

"Unexperienced and frightened, Captain May chose to run and turned his plane back toward British territory."

"Acting against his own directives, Manfred left his squadron and continued his pursuit."

"Australian soldiers opened fire from the ground and..."

"...a single bullet, shot from behind, passed diagonally through his chest."

"Manfred Von Richthofen, the Red Baron, crashed into a field alongside the road from Corbie to Bray."

"Although the Allies did not fly at night..."

"It was all the time required for my little pets to take wing and fulfill my commands."

"Many patrols on long range sorties often did not return to their airfields until dusk."

AIEEE!

HURRY!
LAY HER
DOWN!

WHAT IS WRONG
WITH THE
MISTRESS?

I DON'T KNOW. QUICKLY,
FETCH ME SOME WATER
AND CLEAN TOWELS.
I HAVE TO CLEAN
HER UP.

RIGHT
AWAY,
IRENA.

OH, MISTRESS,
WHAT ARE WE
TO DO?

"I could hear Irena's words as though
through a thick fog that had enveloped
me. Draining me of all my strength."

I DO NOT KNOW. BUT IF IT WERE TRUE. IF GOD ALLOWED THIS LIFE TO COME INTO YOU...

YES! YES! GO ON, WOMAN, SAY IT!

THEN IT WOULD MEAN THE END OF YOUR LIFE AS IT IS.

YOU COULD NOT CONCEIVE A CHILD WITHOUT SACRIFICING YOUR IMMORTALITY.

YOU MEAN, I WOULD BE MORTAL. BUT HOW CAN WE BE SURE? I MUST KNOW.

THERE ARE WAYS. VERY OBVIOUS ONES.

SUCH AS?

HERE. TASTE MY BLOOD.

NO!

I'M GOING TO BE SICK AGAIN.

103

I WAS RIGHT! MISTRESS, YOU CANNOT EVEN STAND THE SIGHT OF BLOOD.

DON'T YOU SEE? THE CHANGE HAS ALREADY BEGUN.

YOU SAID THERE WERE OTHER WAYS. WHAT ARE THEY? I MUST BE SURE.

THEN, MISTRESS, COME WITH ME TO FACE THE DAWN.

YES, OF COURSE, THE ULTIMATE TEST. BUT I MUST GO ALONE.

PRAY FOR ME.

"Thus I started the long walk to the roof."

Re--Imagining a Classic Vamp

This particular story came about because of my love of the old Universal monsters; Frankenstein, Dracula and the Wolf Man. As a teenager growing up in the

1960s, I saw these black and white horror classics on those late night creature-features that were so prevalent around the country. After screening the big three, the networks would often follow up with all the sequels that were made. I forget just how many Frankenstein films there were all total, never mind the ones where Dracula and the Wolf Man would show up. As a kid, I loved seeing my favorite monsters all together in one film.

With the advent of video recorders, I began amassing a huge collection of movies. During this process, I came across the sequel to Dracula. It was called DRACULA'S DAUGHTER and was released from Universal in 1936, the year after DRACULA. Apparently, as the story goes, the success of DRACULA had the studio scrambling to do a sequel. Sadly, actor Bela Lugosi, who had been playing the blood-sucker on stage for many years prior to his screen adaptation, was tired of the role. Happy with the success of the movie, he hoped it would offer him other opportunities for different roles. He turned down the offer to do the sequel.

Although a setback, the studio remained undaunted in its plans to produce another vampire classic. The writers came up with the idea of centering the new film on Dracula's heir, a ravishingly beautiful, exotic daughter. It begins where the first film ended with the Countess Marya Zaleska arriving in England just after the count's defeat at the hands of Prof. Abram Van Helsing. She has her father's remains cremated and then establishes herself as an avant-garde artist in a studio apartment in London. All too soon Marya's finds herself craving blood and soon begins preying on night people of the city.

Brunette Gloria Holden, a relatively unknown bit player, landed the role of Marya and she was absolutely perfect in it. Possessing a haughty, mysterious beauty, she commanded every scene she is on camera. Including a daring, erotic moment when she seduces a young London prostitute. It is a sexually charged scene that most fans have never

forgotten, including this writer. The plot revolved around her attempts to cure herself of her affliction and in doing so she falls in love with a psychiatrist played by Otto Kruger. By the end of the movie, he learns her true nature and aids the authorities in destroying her.

Many fans and film critics to this day consider DRACULA'S DAUGHTER superior to its predecessor. It is one of my all time favorites and I watched it often, now on DVD. I always hoped to someday do something with this truly wonderful character. What would eventually spur my imagination into action was another movie; the 2001 Universal remake of THE MUMMY. This re-interpretation of yet another classic monster by writer/director Stephen Sommers was sheer genius.

Sommers, rather than modernizing the original, chose to keep it in the 1930s. He merged the horror plot with a fast-action Indiana Jones type adventure. In watching it for the first time, it was obvious that Brandon Fraser, as the wise-cracking soldier-of-fortune looking for lost treasure, was another version of Indy. And as we all know, that blending of genres was a whopping success at the box office. And it certainly got my head moving in the right direction.

If I were to re-do DRACULA'S DAUGHTER, in what period would I set it in to provide a completely different atmosphere to a gothic horror piece? As I mentioned earlier, in the original, Marya fell in love with a head-shrink. What if she were to fall in love with someone a whole lot more interesting? Someone handsome, daring and real?

Which is where another interest of mine comes in. I am a flying enthusiast and no chapter of aviation history intrigues me more than that of its role in World War One. It was in this conflict that combat took to the skies and aerial warfare was born. Stories of those brave, chivalrous pilots and their amazing dogfights in the skies over Europe never ceased to thrill me. Especially the exploits of Germany's greatest ace, Manfred Von Richthofen, better known as the Red Baron.

What if Marya met Von Richthofen and they had a torrid love affair set against the backdrop of World War One? That one idea became the nucleus of what would become a four year journey to this publication.

As I began to see the dramatic potential of such a tale, I began accumulating biographical data on the Red Baron. Eventually I was able to write up an historical time-table from the day he joined the armed forces, first as an infantryman, to his becoming a pilot, his country's greatest ace, up to his death. Since Von Ricthofen was a real historical figure, I wanted to keep the data regarding his war service completely accurate.

I wove the fiction part, his encounter with the beautiful vampire and subsequent affair, around that history.

It was an easy script to write. I had been germinating these concepts in my head for years and finally getting them down on paper was exhilarating. The script took me approximately six months to complete. Once done, I began trying to interest various comic publishers and had absolutely no luck whatsoever. Then a very strange thing happened. The more I talked about the concept to friends and colleagues, the more they suggested I turn it into a movie script. They saw it as a movie. I loved the idea and put finding a comic publisher on hold while I sat down to write my story a second time. Thus another six months passed and when finished, I had what I still believe to be a damn good property.

But it was a property I could still not interest publishers or studios in. Somewhere during the next year, I hooked up with Rob Davis, a comic colleague I'd met many years ago when we were both affiliated with Now Comics. I'd wanted to do a project with Rob, as he is a gifted graphic storyteller. We put a few proposals together back then, but luck wasn't with us and none of them found a home. So here we were, some twenty years later getting caught up with each other's lives and careers. Somewhere in all that, I mentioned DAUGHTER OF DRACULA (my new version of the title) and Rob asked to see the comic script. After reading it, he told me he liked it a great deal and would be interested in doing it; meaning the works, pencils, inks and letters. But there was one problem. He couldn't promise to give me more than one page a week. That meant he would need 108 weeks, over two full years, to do it.

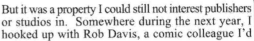

Considering that I'd been sitting on it for two years already, and no one was knocking down my door to buy it…and Rob was the one artist I knew could do my story justice, I said, "Okay." He was surprised and happy. True to his word, he delivered one stunning page every single week for the next two years! Talk about dedication and commitment to a project. And it shows in every single one of these beautiful and powerful pages. Rob brought DAUGHTER OF DRACULA to life in ways I had only dreamed of. So much so, that it now belongs to both of us equally, and finally, to you, our readers. We thank you for buying this and we hope sincerely that it has entertained you.

It was a joy for us to do, more so because of the hard work and time it took to complete. Will it ever become a film? What do you think? Rob and I, we're willing to wait, you see, we're really a couple of patient dudes.

Ron Fortier
Fall 2007
Somersworth, NH

Early Character Sketches

Baron Manfred Von Richthofen

Countess Marya Dracula

WELCOME TO CAPE NOIRE

Located on the Northwest Coast, Cape Noire is a booming economic giant whose inner core has been corrupted by all manner of evil. From the sadistic mob bosses who ruthlessly control vast criminal empires to the fiendish creatures that haunt its maze of back alleys, Cape Noire is a modern Babylon of sin and depravity.

Amidst this den of iniquity strides a macabre warrior committed to avenging the innocent and holding back the tide of villainy. He is *Brother Bones, the Undead Avenger* and there is no other like him. A one-time heartless killer, he is now the spirit of vengeance trapped in an undying body. He is the unrelenting sword of justice as meted out by his twin .45. automatics

His face, hidden forever behind an ivory white skull mask, is the entrance to madness for those unfortunate enough to behold it. This new prose collection features five suspenseful, fast-paced, action-packed stories featuring pulp fiction's most original hero, Bother Bones. Time to draw the shades, light the candles and enter into a Tapestry of Blood.

Daughter of Dracula™

SCRIPT:
RON FORTIER
AIRSHIP27@COMCAST. NET

ART/DESIGN:
ROB DAVIS
ROB_M_DAVIS@EXCITE.COM

COVER ART:
MARK MADDOX

REDBUD STUDIO

Daughter of Dracula,
Graphic Novel.
Published by Redbud Studio comics.
5200 E. Mt. Zion Church Rd.
Hallsville, MO 65255

All rights reserved. Daughter of Dracula, it's logo, all related
characters are © & ™ 2014 Ron Fortier. Interior art is © 2014
Rob Davis. Cover art © 2007 Mark Maddox.

ISBN-13: 978-0692260913
ISBN-10: 0692260919

Second Edition

Printed in the United States of America

10 9 8 7 6 5 4 3 2 1

Made in the USA
Middletown, DE
28 March 2024

51873520R00064